The
Storm Lion
OF
PENZANCE

CORNWALL EDITIONS LIMITED

FOWEY

Cornwall Editions Limited
8 Langurtho Road
Fowey
Cornwall PL23 1EQ
UK

www.cornwalleditions.co.uk

Publisher: Ian Grant

This edition first published in the United Kingdom,
the USA and Canada in 2005

ISBN 1-904880-03-7

Typeset in Times and Sabon
Designed by Kim Lynch

Printed in China
Papers used by Cornwall Editions are natural, recyclable products
made from wood grown in sustainable forests;
the manufacturing processes conform to
the environmental regulations of the country of origin

1 3 5 7 9 10 8 6 4 2

The author wishes gratefully to acknowledge provision of archival material by the staff of the Morrab Library and of Penlee House in Penzance.

For my father, a Camborne man who shared with me both lion and storm; and for Pat who loved the story.

THE Storm Lion OF PENZANCE

Once a boy called Thomas lived in the heart of England, surrounded by grassy hills and fields of corn.

When Thomas was only nine years old his father died of a fever. After this, it grew bleak in the cottage where Thomas lived with his mother, Mary. Without the money that Thomas' father had earned working on farms, there was no coal in the grate and no food in the cupboard.

"Thomas," said his mother after many weeks, "we have to leave this place and go away."

"We can't go away!" Thomas exclaimed. "This is home!"

"We've become poor," said Thomas' mother with a sigh. "I cannot pay the rent for the cottage. My brother William lives in the town of Penzance. He's a fisherman and he'll take you out in his boat."

"But I don't know anything about fishing!" said Thomas. "I don't want to live by the sea!"

"We have to go," said his mother. "In Penzance, we'll make a new home."

"I don't want a new home!" Thomas said.

His mother hugged him. "Sometimes we can't stop change from happening," she said. "But you'll see, Thomas. Things will get better."

Thomas and his mother packed their clothes, and set out on their long journey. Sometimes walking, sometimes riding in wagons, they travelled through England, south and west, to where Cornwall stuck out into the blue Atlantic like a rocky toe.

After many days they came to the town of Penzance, its grey houses facing the wind and water. Thomas stared around. He had never seen the sea before. It frightened him, with its rushing waves and changing tides. It was nothing like the grassy fields at home. He felt dizzy from all the changes in his life and the hunger in his belly.

Thomas and his mother moved into Uncle William's cottage. Uncle William was a big man with red cheeks. He squeezed Thomas' shoulder in

welcome, and his wide smile made Thomas feel warm.

The morning came for Thomas' mother to begin work in the pilchard sheds, layering fish and salt into barrels. "You go down to the beach and help your uncle," she said, wrapping her shawl around her head.

Thomas dawdled in narrow streets. He peered into shop windows at hot pasties and saffron buns, coils of rope and fishermen's boots. Everything seemed so strange. He tried to forget that Uncle William was waiting but, everywhere Thomas went, the sound and taste of the sea followed. The wind was flavoured with salt and steamed crab. It carried around the stories old men told, of fast ships and enormous waves. It lifted up the voices of women, sharp as seagull cries. "Fresh mackerel, fine mackerel!" they called.

It was impossible for Thomas to forget about the sea or about Uncle William's boat on the beach. As dark clouds covered the afternoon sun, Thomas trudged to the water. The tide was out and nets dried on the sand. He went down the steps in the sea wall, watching the waves. The sea was - huge! It stretched to the edge of the world and seemed to turn into sky. And the sea was - alive! It was like a big dangerous animal, breathing and moving.

Uncle William's boat, Mary Rose, lay on the shingle. Uncle William was spreading tar over her hull.

"Give us a hand, me 'andsome," he said.

Thomas dipped a long-handled brush into the sticky tar and began to spread it over the boat. A dark smell filled his nose. Tar dripped onto his arms and smeared on his knees.

"If you get any more tar on you, you'll be as water-tight as the boat," teased Uncle William. His smile wrinkled his blue eyes, making Thomas feel happier than he had since his father died.

"Tomorrow, you'll be ten years old," said Uncle William. "Almost a man. 'Tez time I started to make a fisherman of you."

Thomas didn't feel like almost a man. When he thought of sailing over the strange water in the Mary Rose, he went as cold as if winter had arrived. Beside his big fear, he shrank smaller and smaller.

"I'll teach you everything I know about the sea," promised Uncle William.

Thomas' mother said that Uncle William could find fish in a thick mist, and safe harbour in pitch darkness. Uncle William will keep me safe, thought Thomas - but still he wanted to run away from the mysterious sea.

"Uncle," he said, "I have to go home for supper."

"Get along then," said Uncle William kindly.

Thomas panted up the steps onto the sea wall. He jogged along the top and came to a statue of a proud, sitting lion. Thomas stroked his hand over the lion's salty bronze sides. He climbed on the lion's back and it grew warm under his legs. In the strange town, the lion seemed like a friend.

"I don't want to be a fisherman," Thomas whispered into the lion's smooth ears.

He didn't know where to find the courage he needed.

The wind was rising. It buffeted Thomas as he slid off the lion's back and ran home to his mother.

"Your uncle caught these mackerel," she said, flipping fish in the pan. Thomas wrinkled his nose. Even in his own home, he couldn't escape the sea.

"Soon, you'll be a fisherman too," said his mother proudly. "William is a fine sailor. He carries winds and waves in his head, like a map."

Thomas' food stuck in his throat.

"Think what a help you'll be, Thomas," said his mother. "The fish you catch, and the money you earn, will put food on the table and oil in the lamp."

Thomas hung his head. If only he could help some other way.

After supper, Thomas escaped out into the blustery wind that threw salt spray against his cheeks. He carried scraps for the stray cat that waited at the door. It rubbed golden fur against Thomas' knee and purred. Thomas wished it belonged to him.

Overhead, a window creaked open and Mr. Trelawney, the artist living upstairs, looked out.

"You're the new nephew," he said. "Come and visit me."

Mr. Trelawney's rooms smelled of turpentine, and beside one window stood a beautiful telescope.

"Today," said Mr. Trelawney, as he cleaned brushes, "I saw you sitting on a lion. Do you know that lions come from hot, grassy places?"

That lion is just like me, thought Thomas. It's not a sea creature either.

"Maybe the lion is afraid," Thomas said.

"Maybe it doesn't like sitting close to the waves."
Mr. Trelawney waggled his eyebrows in surprise.
"Lions are a symbol of courage," he said.
"And Thomas, think how fortunate your lion is.
Every day it looks at the bright water,
the wonderful light. The sea is so beautiful
that I never grow tired of painting it."
Thomas stared at Mr. Trelawney. When
Uncle William talked about the sea, he spoke
only of tides and currents, rocks and fish.
He never spoke of beauty and light.
Mr. Trelawney closed the lid on his box of
brushes, and Thomas went outside. Uncle
William had given him a hoop to chase
through the streets. The wind was growing
stronger. It tossed the seagulls around while
storm clouds rushed in from the west
like shoals of frightened fish.

Thomas' hoop spun downhill faster than he could catch it. He dashed after it to the sea wall. Angry waves thundered on the beach and dragged pebbles to and fro. White horses galloped on every wave. Thomas stared in horror. He grabbed his hoop off the wet cobbles, then turned to hurry home to safety.

A group of men huddled on a street corner. "Hey boy! Come here and help!" one of them called.

Thomas pretended he hadn't heard, and kept his back turned.

"Hey boy!" the voice shouted again. Thomas plodded over to the men, keeping his eyes fixed on the wild water. He didn't want to come close to it.

"Look there!" The man pointed. "Tell us what your young eyes see."

Thomas squinted into the wind. "It's a boat," he answered.

"What boat is it?"

Thomas squinted harder in the stormy light. "It's the Mary Rose!" he gasped.

"She's torn loose from her moorings," another man shouted. "The wind has her!"

"She's heading for the rocks!" a third man yelled. "She'll be wrecked!"

"She's my Uncle William Boscawen's boat," Thomas said.

"Run, boy! Run for your uncle! He's in The Dolphin having a pint."

Thomas stood still, staring at the Mary Rose. She pitched and tossed in the heavy waves as white water burst against her hull. If I don't save her, Thomas thought, I won't have to go to sea. She'll be wrecked and I can stay at home.

Then he thought of his mother, who needed money for food. He thought of Uncle William's big smile, and how he shared his cottage with them. Thomas knew that he must try to save the Mary Rose because of the people he loved.

"Run boy, run!" He dropped his hoop, doubled his fists, and began to run along the sea wall towards The Dolphin pub.

A huge wave whooshed out of the dark. Thomas crouched in terror as it crashed into the wall. Cold, hard spray fell around him. With a sob, he bolted into the doorway of a house for shelter. Then bravely he stepped out and forced his legs forward. Another huge wave crashed into the wall. Fear turned Thomas into a statue. His legs wouldn't move. He couldn't go forward or even turn back to shelter.

It felt as if he stood on the sea wall for hours. He knew the Mary Rose was groaning in the storm. Soon she would be wrecked because he was afraid. She was named after Thomas' mother but soon her name, painted in red, would be smashed to splinters. Tomorrow, her broken planks would wash ashore and be burned in fire places. It would be his fault.

"Help!" cried Thomas desperately. "Help!'

In the darkness ahead of Thomas, the lion sat and stared over the waves. It had weathered many storms, though it was a creature of the grasslands.

Thomas thought of the lion with all his might. He pushed one foot forward, then the other. The lion pressed against his leg.

Through his soaked trousers, Thomas felt its golden warmth. "Are you here?" he whispered. He twined his fingers through the lion's tough, salty mane. The lion's warmth spread through his whole body, and strength flowed into him.

When Thomas began to run, the lion moved beside him, stretching out big paws. Wind screamed against Thomas, but he could hear the lion's purr - a rough sound, like the stray cat made. When Thomas' legs began to ache, the lion helped him along. Once he slipped, but he pulled himself up by the lion's mane. Together, they ran through the storm to Uncle William.

At The Dolphin's door, Thomas let go of the lion. "Uncle!" he gasped as he stumbled inside. "It's the Mary Rose. She's drifting onto the rocks!"

"God help us!" cried Uncle William. He snatched his coat and ran out. Other men followed. They were all men who knew the sea and would help save the Mary Rose. Outside, they lit their lanterns and shouted instructions. Thomas watched admiringly. Their faces showed no fear in the flickering light.

As the lanterns bobbed downhill, Thomas reached out and felt for the lion. He wrapped his fingers into its mane again, and together they ran after the men.

It was dusk now. The moon shone between clouds like a silver penny. Thomas crept towards the sea wall where the men were gathered, water splashing around their boots. Slower and slower, Thomas crept towards the fierce, angry sea. Then he felt the lion press against him. He took a deep breath, and strode forwards. In a moment, he was surrounded by wet coats and strong hands.

Uncle William and another man hauled on a rope, pulling a small boat against the sea wall. Uncle William went to the steps in the wall.

"No, no!" Thomas shouted in terror. But the wind whipped his shout away.

Uncle William went carefully down, gripping the hand rail. Men followed him. At the bottom, Uncle William waited while the sea swirled against his feet. He waited until the little boat lifted up on a wave. Then, neat and quick, Uncle William stepped into the little boat and sat down. One after the other, the men followed him.

They pulled out the oars. "Cast off!" shouted Uncle William over the wind. "Untie the knot, Thomas!"

Thomas was standing beside where the rope was tied to an iron ring. His numb fingers tugged at the wet knot. Below, the wild water played with Uncle William and the boat full of men. He knew that soon the waves would toss the boat against the wall and smash it to pieces. Then Uncle William, with his kind smile, would be in the water fighting for his life.

Hurry, hurry, Thomas told his fingers.

The knot came undone. Thomas hurled the rope towards Uncle's boat and a man caught it. The men began to row. The boat spun away from the wall, and headed into the waves. It climbed up them, and slid down the other sides. It didn't tip or sink. Thomas watched, fascinated. The men rowed in time, all the oars dipping and swinging, stronger than the force of the waves. The little boat headed across the water to the dark shadow of the Mary Rose.

"They'll never make it," someone muttered. "It's too late."

Thomas looked where the water boiled white over the rocks. The Mary Rose drifted closer to them. Any minute now, she would be wrecked.

"Come on!" shouted Thomas. "You can do it, Uncle William!"

Closer and closer the little boat crept to the Mary Rose. Now the boats were side by side, rising and falling in the waves. Between the boats was a crack of water. If anyone fell into that, he would be a dead man.

Thomas bit his lip and stopped breathing.

Uncle William waited until a wave lifted the little boat. Up and up it was tossed, alongside the Mary Rose. When the little boat was as high as her gunwhale, Uncle William leapt over the black crack like a lion leaping from one rock to another. He landed safely in his boat.

"Hurrah!" cheered Thomas and the men on the wall.

Two more men leaped into Uncle William's boat. The sail flapped up the mast. Slowly, the Mary Rose turned away from the rocks. Uncle William was at the tiller, swinging her bows towards safety.

"He's taking her to Newlyn harbour," one of the men on the wall said.

Thomas let his breath out in a long sigh.

"I didn't think he'd make it," another man said.

"Nor he wouldn't have - but for this boy here," someone else replied.

The men looked at Thomas admiringly and one gave him a friendly thump on the back.

"Well done, me 'andsome," a man said. "If you hadn't run so fast, your uncle would have lost his boat."

Thomas straightened his back. As the men headed towards their cottages, he felt in the darkness for the lion. He had forgotten all about it, and now it was gone. Thomas smiled. I was wrong about the lion, he thought. It's not afraid of the waves at all.

Then he ran home, his tired legs staggering over the cobbles.

At the cottage door, Mr. Trelawney was stroking the stray cat. "Why Thomas," he said, "you look worn out. What have you been doing?"

Thomas tried to answer but his teeth chattered.

"Let your mother know you're home," said Mr. Trelawney. "Put some dry clothes on, then come and talk to me."

When Thomas climbed the stairs a few minutes later, Mr. Trelawney handed him a cup of hot chocolate. It was delicious! It warmed Thomas from his toes to his ears.

Sitting on Mr. Trelawney's painting stool, Thomas told about the rescue of the Mary Rose. "The lion helped me," he said.

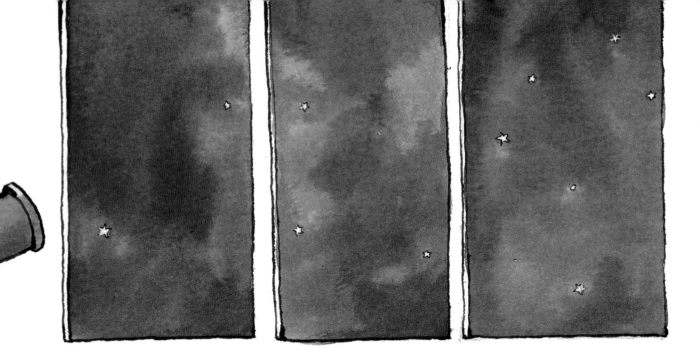

Mr. Trelawney stared at Thomas for a moment. "Come to the window," he said. "Here's a birthday gift, a day early."

"What is it?" asked Thomas with a puzzled frown.

"It's a constellation of stars," said Mr. Trelawney. "Look out, over the water. Do you see the stars there, in a gap in the clouds?"

Thomas peered through the telescope.

"Those stars are a constellation called Leo," said Mr. Trelawney, "and they make a lion. When you're at sea at night, look upwards. You'll see a lion keeping watch over you in the sky. And remember, Thomas, that anyone can have the brave heart of a lion."

Thomas squinted at Leo for a long time. Then a huge yawn stretched his mouth wide.

"Off to bed with you," said Mr. Trelawney. "Tomorrow the sun will shine. You're a lucky boy, to be sailing over the beautiful sea. You can come home and tell me how to paint it."

Mr. Trelawney was right. In the morning, sunshine sparkled on blue water. Thomas sat up in bed and blinked. His mother was rattling cups in the kitchen.

It's my tenth birthday, Thomas thought. Today, I have to sail on the Mary Rose. Fear shivered through him, until he remembered the lion. Then he felt calm. He whistled as he pulled on his trousers and went into the kitchen.

"Happy Birthday!" said his mother. She handed him a pair of fisherman's socks that she had knitted.

"These will keep you warm until you're home again," she said as she hugged him.

In came Uncle William, his broad shoulders blocking the door. "Happy Birthday!" he called.

Thomas undid the string around Uncle William's paper parcel. He unfolded a sou'wester raincoat and hat and pulled them on. They would keep him dry in the boat.

"You're some fast runner!" boasted Uncle William. "You saved the Mary Rose right enough. I'm proud to take you on board."

Thomas glowed. Being ten made him feel bigger and stronger. After breakfast, he took long strides as he and Uncle William went down to the harbour.

Meow! something cried and Thomas turned around.

The golden cat from outside the cottage door was trotting behind him.

"It's following me!" cried Thomas. "Can I bring it to sea?"

Uncle William scratched his head. The cat meowed again, and Uncle William smiled. "Everybody needs a friend," he said.

Thomas scooped up the cat. It felt as warm as the lion had, and it was purring.

When Thomas stepped over the gunwhale of the Mary Rose, he whispered "Welcome aboard" to the cat. He knew it would be safe with Uncle William and himself. For Uncle William was a man who could set a course in a blind fog; who knew where he was, even in darkness, by the feel of the water under the keel. And Thomas was a boy who had found courage, and knew where Leo roamed the night sky.

As the Mary Rose sailed from Mount's Bay, the statue on the wall stared across the water. The lion would keep faithful watch until Thomas came safely home, bringing fish from the beautiful, blue-green sea.

The End